100 Sassy Animals

2nd book in the Grumpy Animals Series

by

Beastflaps

For my little family.
May they never go hungry.

Every day may not be good, but there's good in every day.

That's how I roll.

Believe in yourself, and you're halfway there.

Do NOT the cat.

I don't sweat, I sparkle.

I don't always bark,
but when I do,
it's for no reason.

I'm a lean, mean eating machine.

Say hello to my little friend.

If you can't handle me at my worst, please don't leave me.

Ain't nobody got time for that!

But first,
let me take a selfie.

Keep calm and carry on.

Sorry, not sorry.

Haters gonna hate.

I have no idea what I'm doing.

Too glam to give a damn.

Resting beach face.

Relationship status:
It's complicated.

I'm not always sarcastic.
Sometimes, I'm sleeping.

I need a six-month vacation, twice a year.

I'm not arguing.
I'm just explaining why I'm right.

Don't grow up, it's a trap!

There's a 99% chance
I don't like you.

I'm not short, I'm just concentrated awesome

Namastay in bed.

I'm not bossy, I just have better ideas.

I'm not lazy, I'm just on energy-saving mode.

Bite me.

I'm not great at advice, but can I interest you in a sarcastic comment?

I'm not saying I'm Wonder Woman, but did you ever see me and her in the same room?

I'm on a seafood diet.
I see food, and I eat it.

I've got 99 problems, but a fish ain't one.

I'm sorry for the mean, awful, accurate things I said.

I'm not antisocial,
I'm anti-stupid.

I put the 'elusive' in 'influencer'

Does it look like I care?

I've peaked.

I'm silently correcting your grammar.

I don't suffer from insanity, I enjoy every minute of it.

I'm not high maintenance,
I just have high standards.

I'm just one stomach flu away from my goal weight.

I'm not a control freak,
but you're doing it wrong.

I'm a social vegan,
I avoid meet.

You said I could borrow it.

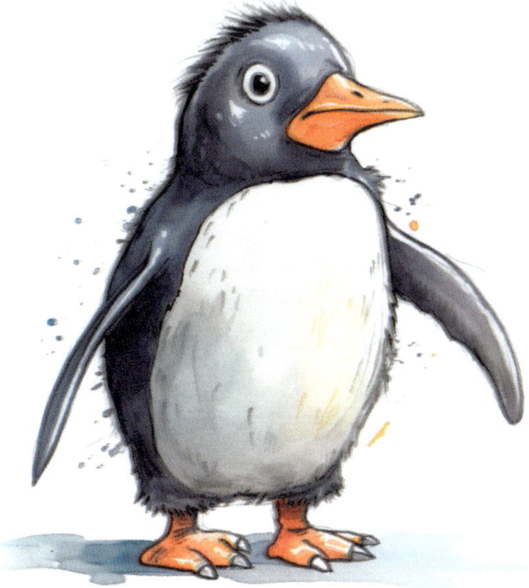

I came, I saw,
I made it awkward.

My life feels like
a test I didn't study for.

I don't have an attitude problem, you have a perception problem.

I'm not weird,
I'm limited edition.

Winter is coming.

I hate multitasking.

Why fit in when you were born to stand out?

Life in the fast lane.

Smile, it's contagious.

I'm a sea cow,
but I identify as a mermaid.

I see dead people.

I'm not shellfish,
I just like to relax.

I'm your knight
in shining armor.

It's not bragging
if you can back it up.

I can't adult today.

I'm not here for the drama, I'm waiting for the snacks

Life moves pretty fast.
Just not for me.

I'm the one who knocks.

I'm not ignoring you,
I'm just prioritizing my naps.

I'm not judging you, I'm just silently disapproving.

I'm not clumsy, I'm just dancing with gravity.

I'm not always right,
but I'm never wrong.

I'm not needy, I just crave attention all the time.

I see what you did there.

You had one job.

Well, that escalated quickly.

Not all heroes wear capes.

I'm not crying, you're crying.

You can't touch this.

Sorry, I can't hear you over the sound of how awesome I am.

I have neither the time nor the crayons to explain this to you.

I would agree with you, but then we would both be wrong.

If at first you don't succeed, then skydiving definitely isn't for you.

If you want to go fast, go alone.
If you want to go far, go with your pack.

In the middle of every difficulty lies opportunity.

It was a calculated risk, but boy do I suck at math

It's always the darkest before you see the light.

life isn't about waiting for the storm to pass, it's about learning to dance in the rain

Life's a journey,
enjoy the ride.

It's not about winning, it's the taking apart that counts.

The only way to do great work is to love what you do.

What lies behind us and what lies before us are tiny matters compared to what lies within us.

When one door closes, another one opens. You just need to scratch at it.

You miss 100%
of the shots you don't take.

Printed in Great Britain
by Amazon